CONTENTS

CHAPTER 1
Scratched! 7

CHAPTER 2
Elfis 12

CHAPTER 3
Case closed . . . .

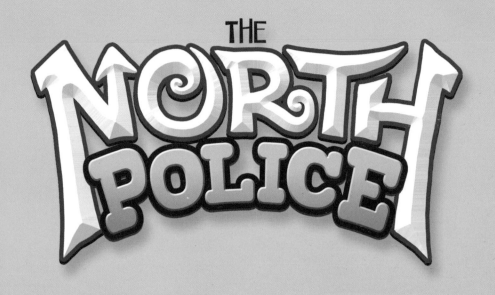

The North Police are

the elves who solve crimes

at the North Pole.

These are their stories...

CHAPTER 1
Scratched!

The Christmas Town

garage is where Santa's sleigh

was stored.

It was also a crime scene!

Santa's sleigh had a huge

scratch on it.

Someone must have taken the sleigh out last night and scraped it on something.

Santa couldn't have taken the sleigh out. He had been in bed with a cold.

So who did it?

The North Police's greatest

detectives were on the case!

As Detective Sugarplum

sipped some egg nog, Detective

Sprinkles got to work.

Sprinkles dusted for prints with icing sugar.

But there were no fingerprints at all.

"Hmm," said Sugarplum, "if someone rode the sleigh last night, they would have left prints. Let's talk to the elf who called about the crime."

Eve's job was to look after Santa's sleigh.

"What can you tell us, Eve?" asked Sugarplum.

"Only one elf was near the garage," Eve said. "Elfis."

CHAPTER 2
Elfis

Elfis was the coolest elf in Christmas Town.

The North Police found him rocking out on his electric bell at a local Christmas club.

"You were seen near the

garage last night," said

Detective Sprinkles.

"I'm not talking," Elfis said.

"Then you leave us no

choice," said Sugarplum.

"We're going to have to play good cop, better cop," added Sugarplum.

"Go ahead and try," Elfis said. "Do your best."

"Maybe this will change

your mind," said Sprinkles.

He offered Elfis a delicious

bag of jelly beans.

"Ooh, I love jelly beans!"

cried Elfis.

"If you want the beans, you'll have to spill the beans," explained Sugarplum.

"I admit it," said Elfis, grabbing the jelly beans. "I did it! I lost Mrs Claws!"

"What are you talking about?" asked Sprinkles.

"Mrs Claws is Santa's cat. I was supposed to look after her," said Elfis. "Only I lost her! I thought I saw her near the garage. I went there to look for her."

"So you didn't take the sleigh out for a ride?" asked Detective Sprinkles.

"No!" said Elfis.

"Looks like we're out of clues." Sprinkles sighed.

"I don't think so," said Sugarplum. "I think Elfis has just given us another one!"

CHAPTER 3
Case closed

The detectives returned to

the scene of the crime.

"I bet the sleigh was

scratched on the North Pole,"

said Sprinkles. "That pole is

very pointy!"

"But I don't understand how someone could have taken the sleigh out of the garage last night without being seen," Sprinkles said.

"I don't think anyone took the sleigh out," said Sugarplum.

"Then how did it get scratched on the North Pole?" asked Sprinkles.

"It wasn't scratched by

the North Pole," replied

Sugarplum. "Was it, girl?"

"Um, I'm not a girl,"

replied a very confused

Detective Sprinkles.

"No, you're not," said

Detective Sugarplum, "but she

is!" Sugarplum reached behind

the sleigh and pulled out ...

a cat!

It was Mrs Claws!

"You scratched the sleigh,"
said Detective Sugarplum
as she petted the cat, "didn't
you, girl?"

"Meow," said Mrs Claws.

"Another case neatly wrapped up!" the detectives exclaimed.

The North Police had done it again!

Santa was feeling better and was happy that the case had been solved. He was even happier to have his cat back.

Santa gave Mrs Claws a jolly old hug.

"Achooo!" he sneezed.

"Sir," said Sprinkles, "maybe you're allergic to cats."

"Another mystery for the North Police!" said Sugarplum.

2.2 _____

2.0 _____

1.8 _____

1.6 _____

1.4 _____

1.2 _____

1.0 _____

0.8 _____

CASE 003   NORTH POLICE

MRS CLAWS

Cat • Height 0.6 m • Weight 8 kg

GLOSSARY

allergic have a reaction to animals, dust, pollen, food or other things that can cause sneezing, rashes or other symptoms

detective someone who investigates crimes

egg nog drink made of eggs beaten with sugar and milk or cream

scene place where something bad or mysterious took place

sleigh sledge usually pulled by horses or other animals

These are their stories...

Computer Meltdown

Meet the South Police

The Mystery of Santa's Sleigh

Reindeer Games

only from RAINTREE!

AUTHOR

Scott Sonneborn has written many books, a circus (for Ringling Bros. Barnum & Bailey) and lots of TV programmes. He's been nominated for one Emmy and spent three amazing years working at DC Comics. He lives in Los Angeles, USA, with his wife and their two sons.

ILLUSTRATOR

Omar Lozano lives in Monterrey, Mexico. He has always been crazy about illustration, constantly on the lookout for awesome things to draw. In his spare time, he watches lots of films, reads fantasy and sci-fi books and draws! Omar has worked for Marvel, DC, IDW, Capstone and many other publishers.